Passionate About Pizza
Volume I

Discover the Natural Health Benefits of this Ancient Food

By Canadian Pizza Baking Champion Diana Coutu

Order this book online at www.trafford.com
or email orders@trafford.com

Most Trafford titles are also available at major online book retailers.

Note for Librarians: A cataloguing record for this book is available from Library and Archives Canada at www.collectionscanada.ca/amicus/index-e.html

Printed in Victoria, BC, Canada.

ISBN: : 978-1-4251-7037-0 (soft)

ISBN: : 978-1-4251-7038-7 (ebook)

Our mission is to efficiently provide the world's finest, most comprehensive book publishing service, enabling every author to experience success. To find out how to publish your book, your way, and have it available worldwide, visit us online at www.trafford.com

Trafford rev. 8/31/2009

 www.trafford.com

North America & international
toll-free: 1 888 232 4444 (USA & Canada)
phone: 250 383 6864 ♦ fax: 812 355 4082

Dedication

To my grandmother Betty and my grandfather Cliff who taught me more about life than I can share here. To my mother Lynn who has always been there to encourage and support me and who saw me through my tumultuous teenage years. You never gave up on me and even accommodated my desire for a puppy. I thank you from the bottom of my heart for helping me to become the person I am.

To my husband, partner and best friend Pierre with whom I've enjoyed sharing both the tough and tender moments of my adult life. I couldn't do what I've done without all your love, support and laughter. Thanks for all the memories and all the laughter.

To all the home pizza chef's in training who have asked for me for tips, tricks, recipes and general advice on how to make this most wonderful, simple, delicious and ancient food. This cookbook is for all of you. Thanks for the questions and interest.

Contents

Introduction

Once upon a time pizza was made with simple, all natural and healthy ingredients. Pizza was the perfect meal, providing a reasonable serving from all four food groups in one hand. An ancient food, traces have been found during archaeological digs in brick ovens in Pompeii and Egypt – civilizations from over 2700 years ago. Made with unleavened bread and leftover bits of meats and vegetables, it was the beginnings of pizza.

Pizziollos', the Italian word for pizza makers, are still highly regarded in Italy. Not so much in North America. Today, the majority of pizzas found in North America are made with heavily processed flours, full fat cheeses or worse fake cheeses and processed meats made with fillers and by-products.

My name is Diana Coutu and I'm on a mission to save North Americans from bad pizzas made with cheap ingredients and fake cheeses. Boring, mediocre and unhealthy pizzas have overtaken the industry and become mainstream. Pizza has, for the most part, rightly been lumped into the 'bad fast food' category. It's my position that the North American population is not under a health crisis, rather it is suffering from a food crisis. What I mean by that is that even when the average North American consumer is trying to make better meal choices, they cannot easily find unrefined, unenriched, unmodified and unprocessed foods. I'm bringing Healthy Back to a food that is practical and in demand by today's busy families. I call this "Stealth Health", a way to sneak in healthful foods that are also great tasting and guilt free.

Origins of the Pie

The actual origin of pizza is still highly debated. Italians lay claim to the birthplace of pizza. When the ruins of Pompeii[1] were unearthed they found brick ovens with bits of flatbread still inside. Pompeii was a city in Italy that dates back to the 7th century BC.

Centuries later a man in Naples made pizzas for the local peasants. Queen Marguerite had heard of how delicious and dynamic this peasant food was. She was so compelled to try one that she sent out a messenger to request the pizzas be brought to her. Well, she was the Queen after all. It caused great shock and distress in the kingdom that she even wanted to eat such a vile food thought to be beneath her, in no way could she go and pick one up herself! So she sent for the much talked about pizza maker to bring her one of his famous pizzas. The pizzaollo was very honoured and created a pizza inspired by the 3 colours of the Italian flag. It was a simple flatbread with red crushed tomatoes, sliced white buffalo mozzarella and 3 green basil leaves placed in the center for aesthetics. He then delivered the pizzas to the Queen and of course she loved them so much that she declared that it was the best food that she'd ever eaten. The pizza maker proclaimed a name for his creation and it became known as the Marguerite pizza, which is still a common menu item in Italy today.

Pizza makers are highly regarded in Italy, it's considered an ancient craft and a learned skill, it's widely respected across the country. Of course you're not going to find a pizza maker that sells his pizza at a '2 for 1' price. And you definitely won't find a pizza maker that sells a '3 for 1' or '4 for 1' or even a '5 for 1'. Italians know that you can't make pizza worth eating with a price like that. That's not to say that you won't ever get a bad pizza in Italy, but they know that life ain't about the quantity, it's all about quality and enjoyment. North American pizza is very different. In North America you don't find the same respect of the pizza maker and for the most part with good reason. I believe that more and more North American consumers are looking for healthier choices in their daily diet and pizza is a food that is practical and in demand by today's busy families.

---

[1] Mount Vesuvius erupted in the year 79 AD and within a matter of days the city and its inhabitants were smothered in toxic ash and killed by the poisonous gas that leaked down the mountainside.

Diana's Definition of Gourmet Pizza

Healthy food made with the best ingredients like low fat cheeses, lean meats, fresh veggies, sauce made from ripe red tomatoes grown in the Sunbelt, whole wheat crusts, white crusts made with unbleached flour. Most crusts are made with enriched flour & canola oil. Some are even made of lard. I recommend Olive oil because it's more beneficial health wise than Canola or vegetable oils plus it adds that great bread flavour.

Guaranteed Quality Spices vs. Cheap Spices

Many spices are grown in 3rd world countries where access to clean water and education about proper food handling are real issues. Villagers typically get paid by the pound so sticks, stones and other foreign matter that I won't completely gross you out with, are mixed in with the spices. The truth is, there's not just a big difference in prices on guaranteed quality spices versus cheap ones. There's also a big difference in the amount of spice per gram. Choose a brand / company working side by side with the villagers to ensure maximum quality and purity of their spices.

When you use the best quality spices recipes require less quantity to create great and satisfying flavours. Plus you can be certain that your recipes will always turn out as intended, every time. We only purchase the best quality of spices at Diana's Gourmet Pizzeria, yet the cost is only 1% of the total cost of the recipes. Most of the flavour is provided by the least expensive price per serving. When you buy the best spices, less is truly more.

Tomato Bases

We start our award winning marinara recipe with grade 'A' premium quality crushed tomatoes that are bright red in the can naturally sweet and full of lycopene, which studies have shown helps to prevent prostate cancer. There are grade 'B' through 'D' quality tomatoes available, which many pizza places use as a base for their sauce.

Lower quality tomatoes are orange & sometimes even brown in the can. The increased acid makes them bitter to the taste, especially compared to the premium grade 'A' tomatoes. Many of these lower grades of canned tomatoes have plastic liners inside the tin cans because the acid from the tomatoes is so strong it will eat the tin and leach tin flavor into the tomatoes.

Pizza places that use low quality tomatoes try to overcome the bitterness and orange colour by loading the sauce with sugar and red dyes to mimic a better quality tomato. I've tasted some pretty bad sauces, some that seem more like cheap ketchup than a pizza sauce.

Real Cheese vs. Fake Cheese

A lot of places that sell pizza mix their dairy cheese with fake cheese. Non dairy cheeses are being used at many chains and low quality independents. Some of these fake cheeses are made from soy, others from oils. I don't have any issues with soy cheeses, in fact I've tried to source good quality ones for a segment of my customers. I do take issue with pizza places using these ingredients but not disclosing it to their customers in an effort to keep prices unrealistically low. Since the 1980's two large pizzas with two toppings are often advertised for $19.99 (or less) and they come with a free 2L. Everything, and I do mean everything; minimum wages, dairy prices, wheat prices, fresh vegetables, top quality meats, real estate, and especially gas prices have gone up since then. The math for mainstream pizza has stayed the same. More and more savvy consumers are questioning how that's possible.

Full Fat Cheese vs. Low Fat Cheese

A lot of pizza places will use a full fat mozzarella sometimes mixing it with low-fat or soy cheese. They do this because the full fat mozzarella adds a lot of flavour, many people find it palatable, but then don't feel well afterwards. Typically, pizza places that use full fat cheese are trying to add flavour to a cardboard tasting crust topped with low quality meats and vegetables. Personally, I can't eat pizza made this way. Rather, I can eat it but my body doesn't digest it well, unless I chase it down with a big bottle of the pink stuff. And that's no way to eat, much less a way to live.

Enriched White Flour vs. Unbleached Flour vs. 100% Whole Wheat vs. Whole Grain

Many pizza crust recipes are made with enriched white flour, which on the surface sounds like a good thing, but the fact is that it's not. When your digestive system breaks down enriched white flour it becomes sugar which gives you some energy, however it doesn't provide you with many nutrients and also leaves you still feeling hungry.

Try to avoid simple carbohydrates like enriched white flours and refined grains.

North American diets are severely lacking in fiber. Fiber comes from whole wheat, whole grain and multi-grain breads. Fiber takes longer for your digestive system to break down and as a result leaves you feeling fuller longer. It is also a source of complex carbohydrates (starches) and a major source of B vitamins, magnesium and many other minerals.

Health

The following section discusses the healthful benefits of common and not so common ingredients found on pizzas.

Artichokes: A good source of folate, vitamin C and potassium. They are also low in calories and high in fiber.

Asparagus: A good low-calorie source of folate and vitamins A and C.

Avocados: A rich source of folate, vitamin A and potassium. Useful amounts of protein, iron, magnesium and vitamins C, E, and B_6. Very high in calories, 85% coming from fat.

Beans: High in folate and vitamin A and C. Mature (shelled) beans are high in protein and iron.

Bean Sprouts: Some are high in folate; others are fair to good sources of protein vitamin C, B vitamins and iron.

Broccoli: An excellent source of vitamin C, a good source of vitamin A and folate. Significant amounts of protein, calcium, iron and other minerals. Rich in bioflavonoids and other plant chemicals that protect against cancer. Low in calories and high in fiber.

Brussels Sprouts: An excellent source of vitamin C. A good source of protein, folate, vitamin A, iron and potassium. Contain bioflavonoids and other substances that protect against cancer.

Carrots: An excellent source of beta carotene, the precursor of vitamin A. A good source of dietary fiber and potassium. Helps prevent night blindness and may help lower blood cholesterol levels and protect against cancer.

Cauliflower: An excellent source of vitamin C. A good source of folate and potassium. Low in calories and high in fiber.

Cheese: High in protein and calcium. A good source of vitamin B12. Helps to remove plaque from teeth, cheddar and other aged cheeses may alsofight tooth decay. Choose low fat cheeses under 22% milk fat and add a small amount of a higher fat cheese, like Havarti for maximum flavour. A study at the Smell & Taste Treatment & Research Foundation in Chicago showed the smell of cheese pizza increased romantic interest in men by 5%.

Chilies: An excellent source of vitamins A and C. May help nasal congestion. May help prevent blood clots that can lead to a heart attack or stroke. Be careful handling during preparation to prevent irritation of the skin and eyes. May irritate hemorrhoids in susceptible people.

Corn: A good source of folate and thiamine. A fair amount of vitamins A and C, potassium and iron.

Cranberries: A fair source of vitamin C and fiber. Contain bioflavonoids, thought to protect eyesight and help prevent cancer.

Eggplants: Low in calories (unless cooked in fat). While their meaty flavour and texture lends itself to vegetarian dishes they provide minimal nutrients.

Eggs: An excellent source of protein, vitamin B12 and many other nutrients.

Fennel: An excellent source of vitamins A and C (especially the leaves). A good source of potassium, calcium, and iron. High in fiber and low in calories.

Fish: An excellent source of complete protein, iron and other minerals. Some are high in vitamin A. Contains omega-3 fatty acids.

Garlic: May help lower high blood pressure and elevated blood cholesterol. May prevent or fight certain cancers. Antiviral and antibacterial properties help fight infection. May alleviate nasal congestion.

Leeks: A good source of vitamin C, with lesser amounts of niacin and calcium.

Legumes: Contains more protein than any other plant-derived food. A good source of starch, B-complex vitamins, iron, potassium, zinc and other essential minerals. Most are high in soluble fiber.

Lettuce and other Salad Greens: Low in calories and high in fiber. Some varieties are high in beta carotene, folate, vitamin C, calcium, iron and potassium.

Mangoes: An excellent source of beta carotene and vitamins C. A good source of vitamin E and niacin. High in potassium and iron, low in calories, high in fiber.

Mushrooms and Truffles: Fat-free and very low in calories. Rich in minerals. High glutamic acid content may boost immune function.

Olives: High in monounsaturated fats, which benefit blood cholesterol levels. A modest low-calorie source of vitamin A, calcium and iron.

Onions: The green tops are a good source of vitamin C and beta carotene. May lower elevated blood cholesterol and help lower blood pressure. Reduce the ability of the blood to clot. Mild antibacterial effect may help prevent superficial infections.

Peas and Pea Pods: A good source of vitamins A and C, thiamine, riboflavin and potassium. High in pectin and other types of fiber. Provides complete protein when served with grain products.

Peppers: An excellent low-calorie source of vitamin A and C. Red Peppers are loaded with beta carotene. Hot banana peppers and Jalapeno peppers help boost the immune system.

Pineapples: A good source of vitamin C with useful amounts of vitamin B6, folate, thiamine, iron and magnesium.

Pork: Fresh, lean pork is a good source of high-quality protein and B vitamins.

Poultry: An excellent source of protein. Lower in saturated fat than red meats. A good source of vitamin A, the B vitamins, and minerals.

Shellfish: A low-fat source of high-quality protein. A rich source of minerals, including calcium, fluoride, iodine, iron and zinc. A good source of the B-group vitamins.

Spinach: A rich source of vitamin A and folate. High in vitamin C and potassium. A vegetarian source of protein. Contrary to popular belief, spinach is not an essentially good source of iron.

Tofu and other Soy Products: A vegetarian source of high-quality protein and iron. A good source of B vitamins, calcium, potassium, zinc and other minerals. May protect against heart disease and some forms of cancer. Low in calories and fat.

Tomatoes: A useful source of vitamins A and C, folate and potassium. A good source of lycopene, an antioxidant that protects against some cancers.

Zucchini: Low in calories. A good source of vitamins A, C, and folate.

Water

I gave this a section of its' own because of its great importance to the human body. This simple yet readily available ingredient is paramount to good health and longevity however it is often overlooked and unappreciated. Here I hope to bring attention back to this miracle substance which helps keep your entire body working in its natural state of good health. As a side note, when I say water, I mean water, not pop, not tea/coffee/beer/wine, nor any of the vitamin infused waters, not any liquid – I mean good old fashioned water.

Anyone who has ever dieted has been told to drink 6-8 glasses of water a day, however it's often taught as a method of suppressing the appetite. What's not so well known is most of the time when we feel "hungry", it's our body's way of signaling our brains that we need to replenish the moisture loss from our busy activities. We're thirsty. There's a great book that expands on this which you'll find in the recommended reads section of this book, but the premise goes like this;

Our bodies are made up of mostly water, as much as 80% is said to be water. Our brains also have a high percentage. Every time we walk, talk, eat, speak – even think, we use up that precious supply in our bodies and we need to replenish it daily. If you think about yourself on a cellular level, not just the internal organs, but every living cell of your body functions by moving nutrients in and moving waste out. And if there's no moisture for things to move easily then everything slows down and eventually gets backed up.

Add caffeinated and/or alcoholic drinks to that and we further dehydrate ourselves. Most North Americans do not replenish their daily moisture loss which leads to everything from headaches & migraines to more serious afflictions like diabetes, MS, arthritis and other diseases. If you've ever been brutally hung over, you already know what it feels like to be severely dehydrated, where everything from moving your body to processing thoughts and interacting with others becomes difficult beyond measure.

The other misunderstanding about water is how our bodies use it. After reading the above, you may be tempted to drink 2 liters of water all at once, thinking that you're doing your body a favour. The fact is that your body cannot handle that much water at once and this will only 'flush' through your body, in many cases leaving you feeling even more dehydrated.

Imagine a house plant that has not been watered for a couple of weeks. The soil is loose and brittle, perhaps even exposing the roots of the plant. The outer leaves on the plant are curled up in themselves, and all the leaves are brittle and lifeless. If you simply put it in the kitchen sink and run the tap on full you'll only succeed in stripping away the soil and beating the plant to death. But, if you put water in a spray bottle, and 'spritz' the soil and the plant leaves every 20-40 minutes over the course of a couple of days, you will see the house plant come back to life and the soil able to hold moisture again. Our bodies are the same. Ideally, you should sip water throughout the day; 2-4 ounces at a time and you'll see and feel your body come back to its natural state of wellness.

The second part to the equation is sea salt. Sea salt is not table salt and a good quality sea salt contains a mixture of essential minerals in the correct proportion that closely resembles our body's own chemical make-up. The recommended formula for water and sea salt is to take your body weight and divide it in half –that's the amount (in ounces) of water you need to drink every day. For every quart of water, you need ¼ tsp of sea salt for your body to use the water effectively. I use Nature's Cargo™ Sea Salts at home and in the pizzeria.

Proper Salt Creates Hydrochloric Acid

Hydrochloric acid is made from the hydrolysation of chlorine. The chlorine comes from the essentially balanced sodium chloride we find in a good quality Sea Salt. Those who preach a 'no-salt' diet are incorrect: they should know we are salt based creatures—tears, blood, and sweat are salty! They should say a 'no refined sodium chloride' diet.

How a Salt-Free Diet Can Harm Us

Salt-free is probably more harmful than using the table salt that has caused the problems. Water goes wherever salt goes. If we do not replenish the salt reserves in our bodies, we throw off that vital balance of salt and water that keeps us functioning normally. Your body will begin to secret water more quickly in order to raise the level of sodium concentration in the bloodstream.

Signs of too little salt in the diet may take the form of sweating profusely and loss of appetite, extreme fatigue followed by muscles that become sore and stiff and will twitch. Finally, headaches, insomnia and perhaps convulsions in extreme instances. Without proper salt, the cells cannot regenerate and they have no energy. The cells actually take sodium from the saline fluids within the body. Proper salt replenishes these supplies, denying yourself the proper sea salt worsens every problem in which cell repair rejuvenation must occur to maintain body function. This is the most important biological fact to be considered when talking about Sea Salt and deprived of this vitally balanced saline solution, the cells degenerate and age. We all love and crave salt for a reason, we need it—but common table salt is not 'salt', it's a chemical called sodium chloride.

Did you know?

The Roman Legions were paid in salt, which is where the word 'salary' originated. The middle ages saw salt traded ounce for ounce for pure gold. Makes you think of the saying 'a man worth his salt'.

How did the beer get in the dough?

The inspiration came to me back in 2004 when I was considering my entry for a contest by Canadian Pizza magazine looking for 'Canada's Best Pizza Chef'. Canadians have been enjoying pizza & beer every Friday night (or while watching a hockey or football game) for decades, and I wondered what the crust would taste like if I combined the two.

Why did I decide to use Moosehead™ beer?

Moosehead™ is my husband's favourite beer. While he considers himself to be a connoisseur and has enjoyed a few brands, Moosehead™ is and always has been his favourite, so it was in the fridge at the time that I was playing around with my recipe. I stole some of his stash out of the fridge and brought it to the pizzeria.

At first he was angry and he offered to buy me a really cheap brand, but he gave in when I explained how I wanted the flavour that he loved to come out in the crust. Luckily I only needed 2 small test batches before I came up with what eventually became the winning recipe – which to this day he still enjoys eating and pairing up with a nice cold one.

Lifestyle

Italians have a saying, and as I've made many Italian friends I've heard various degrees of slang for it, but it goes like this; if every day you have a good meal, a good poop, and a good love making session then you have all the best pleasures in life. My friend John D'Ambrosio who holds "U.S.A's Best Pizza Chef 2006 & 2007" says that if you think about how you feel after each of the above, that it really don't get any better than that. He has a point.

I would add to that...

As far as I know, this is the only skin, the only skeleton, the only brain, the only muscular, and circulatory and nervous system that I'll ever have and as such it's precious to me, as it should be. My own personal belief is that my essence, my spirit, my soul is eternal and I will evolve as such when it comes time for that. But, I do know for certain that this is the only body that I occupy at this moment in time and that I, for the most part, have complete control on how I take care of it. I make a point to take the best possible care of myself, body, mind and soul. Laughter and music is for the soul, what food is to the body and what desire and enthusiasm is to the mind.

Breathe – deep breathing

Calms the mind, calms the body, and relaxes everything outer & inner. When you're anxious or scared you shorten your breath which quickens your heart rate, increasing blood pressure. This causes tension on your internal organs. Take 5 minutes a day and do nothing else but concentrate on breathing deeply. Yoga and Pilates use breathing exercises in addition to strength building.

Find the funny

A great laugh relieves tension, releases endorphins and improves your overall outlook of life, reminding you that stressful situations are only temporary. Find the funny. Find something to laugh about every day. Even if it's yourself, even if it's hard at first. Find the funny and laugh about it. Laughter is the best thing that you can do, and it's in your control. I love to laugh, I'm always cracking jokes. Even in the worst of situations I can often find something funny. It's not important that everybody gets it, as long as I do. Besides, there are so many ridiculous things in life; you might as well laugh about them. Whether you have a great day or a crappy day – it really is your decision. Go ahead and try it. Focus only on the funny for 3 days. Watch only comedies, bloopers, anything that's funny. Happiness is a habit. Find the funny.

Pets

Pets are funny. Everyone should have a pet. Dogs and cats are especially funny. I had a dog that I adopted from a shelter named Dino who would rub his body against the couch and the carpet – wait, it's not what you think. He would charge himself all up with static electricity and then he'd come over and touch you to shock you. He would do it over and over again. And I would put wool socks on and charge myself up and chase him and 'shock him' back. We called it our game of shock.

My brother thought we were lunatics, he would never play. He always hollered at Dino 'Dumb rat dog! Stop that!" But that didn't stop Dino from trying to play with him. Or Dino would shock himself by touching his nose to the cold air return duct. He would do that over and over too. It was funny. He was one funny little dog. And he was my dog. I had close to 19 years of funny with my Dino and I know that the outlook I came to have in life is directly related to having him in my life. He was truly an amazing companion. He taught me to always find the funny, even if it's the gross funny. Future volume to contain story of Dino Bambino Rat Dog Terrier; King of the Compost Heap.

Find love

It's there, in everybody's life. You need to love yourself first. You can't fully love another and let another love you until you love yourself first. Some people may say it doesn't matter if you love yourself or not. They don't know what they're talking about. I love who I am. I didn't used to; I grew up wishing that I didn't have freckles, or that I'd be 5'8" (not 5' 2 & ¾"). I was too busy looking at what I didn't like about myself than what I did. A lot of kids do. A lot of grown-ups do too.

Once I shifted the focus to what I liked about myself I found out more about myself. I've learned that you don't need to be perfect at everything all the time; you just gotta be you, be happy being you and try to be the best you that you can be. Forgive yourself for your mistakes, laugh about it, if you can. Learn the lesson and move forward.

Relationships

Life is meant to be shared. That said, there hasn't been a relationship in this world where 2 or more people haven't disagreed or rubbed each other the wrong way every once in a while. Whether it's your best friend, a business partner, a co-worker, your brother/sister, mother or even your spouse; the more time you spend together, the more likely that you're going to disagree at some point. If you don't then one of you is either really good at suppressing their emotions or really good at butt kissing.

These days life can be extremely stressful and you (or they) may not even realize that you're bringing it into the relationship. Something that you may have initially found attractive or cute is now what makes you roll your eyes. When you're in a committed relationship you need to look at that special someone everyday and remember what you love about them and how sweet it is. 'Cuz there are going to be times when that same someone or something drives you batty and you just want to stab them in the eye with a fork! The line between love & hate is very thin and any relationship worth its' weight will cross that line a few times. Focus on the love to bring more of it and to tip the scales in its' favour.

Protect your energy

There are people and things in this life that drain your energy. They drain the good energy and leave you with negative energy. Instead, don't let them in. Don't let them drain you. If you do, you will not find all the good that life has to offer, you won't enjoy your life to the fullest. Remember that it is YOUR LIFE and YOU get to decide what you want included in it.

Walk – Move yourself

Scientific studies show that walking uses more neurons and creates more working pathways between those neurons. Walking actually changes the chemistry in your brain. Walk, don't run. People used to go for a walk to get some fresh air and 'clear their heads', what are they doing now? Walking actually works your internal organs too, the only form of exercise that does. See fitness section.

Stretch – Stretch your body

Bodies become tight and muscles shortened during everyday life. Increase your range of movement and lengthen your muscles by stretching. Lay out on the floor, stretch up and down and stretch. The more flexible you are the less likely to become injured. Yoga, Pilates and Tai Chi all use stretching exercises in addition to strength building.

Portion Size and DIETS

During the 1950's, the average dinner plate was 9". Today it's 12". It's interesting to note that the 30% larger size also directly correlates to the increase in obesity rates in North America. Personally, I never cared for the word "DIET", perhaps because the first 3 letters take prominence in my mind and seem like you've made a commitment to something awful. I prefer "lifestyle adjustment", or even better, "a personal commitment to better health". After years of my own personal struggles with "DIETS" and seeing friends having their results yo-yo, I've come to the conclusion that the majority view on DIETS is wrong.

Restricting what you can and cannot eat for the period of 'the DIET' can only lead to feelings of guilt and shame, i.e.; I can't have that because I'm too fat. Way to go DIET, you've now made me feel like a sack of crap. Health begins in the mind and you cannot change how you see yourself in your mind if every time you think of food you're reminded of the choices of your past. For the best results when you've made a commitment to better health, choose healthy options and smaller portions. Eating smaller, yet more frequently will generally get you the fastest and healthiest weight loss. Eat only enough for the next 2-3 hours so your body can convert stored fat to energy.

Two to three slices of pizza with lean meat (chicken, low fat Capicolla) low fat cheese (you can always go light on the cheese too) and an assortment of vegetables will give your body all the nutrients of the 4 food groups with the added benefit of portion control. And darn it, if you're craving it, go ahead and have that piece of chocolate fudge cake and enjoy it too!

Fitness

Now I'm not a doctor nor do I play one on TV. Always consult a doctor about your health and diet concerns.

Waist Management vs. Weight Management

Throw out your bathroom scale. Get a tape measure. Measure and monitor your waist. Throw out your scale. See lifestyle section.

Move your body. It's important to walk at least 30 minutes a day. Studies show that your brain chemistry changes when you walk. There is a lot more brain activity and tons more neuron connections are created. Why does that matter? Well your brain is a muscle too, and it's perhaps the most important muscle to work out to defend it against Alzheimer's and other diseases of later life.

Walking also works your internal organs; all the blood pumping through your system forces everything to have a good work out. Most people don't think that there are any benefits to walking, that at the very least you need to jog in order to get results. Completely untrue. In fact it's actually more stressful on your body to run rather than walk. Joggers won't tell you that. But it hurts more than it helps, so to say.

Body weight exercises are also very important; Build muscles, anything that isn't used atrophies. That means it shrinks and gets weak. I recommend studying Matt Furey and Eddie Baran both who have very good home study programs like; Hindu squats, bridges, wall chair, and other exercises that don't require travel to gym. More strength, tone, definition, more body control, lean muscles, rather than bulky weight lifting muscles (nicer on women). Wherever you are, you can fit some exercise in your day – unless it's a hotel room in Rome. You're lucky enough if you can fit with your entire luggage in a hotel room in Rome. In cases where the hotel room carpet makes you go 'ewe' lay a towel down or forgo floor exercises all together. Remember that your brain is a muscle too.

Pizza Recipes

How to Use a Pizza Stone

Every pizza cookbook I've read tells you to check the manufacturer's recommendations for use & care of your pizza stone. The problem is that hardly any pizza stones come with instructions, never mind recommendations. You often see them advertised for sale around Christmas with a pizza cutter and maybe a serving plate.

Some books tell you to get an unglazed tile from your local hardware store. Let's just say that I've never had any luck with that route. Off the holiday season your best bet to find a good pizza stone is at a restaurant supply store. I've also had many people tell me that they bought their stone from a 'kitchen supply' home party. Pizza stones are very simple, they're unglazed tile and you'll find them in round or square shapes.

Pizza Stone Basics: How to Use & Care for Your Stone

The first time you use your pizza stone, you should bake it for at least 1 & ½ hours before baking a pizza on it. You want to bake out any impurities in the stone before you start to bake your food on it.

Step 1: Place oven rack on the lowest rack position in your oven. Put the pizza stone on the rack.

Step 2: Preheat both the stone AND the oven at 450°F for 1 hour. It's the stored heat from the stone that cooks your pizza and gives it a great 'dry' bake.

You are ready to cook your pizza.

Your pizza will cook quickly, 7-12 minutes depending on the size and number of toppings. Rotate the pizza 180°, halfway through cooking. The back of your oven is always hotter than the front, so rotate the pizza for even baking.

Some other important tips...

The stone is hot. Be careful not to touch it directly when cooking on it.

The stone stays hot for a while, so you must leave the stone to cool for several hours before moving it or putting it away once you've finished cooking.

Pizza Stone Basics: How to Use & Care for Your Stone (cont)

Never get your stone wet. Because it is unglazed tile, the water will seep into the stone's pores, weakening it.

During regular use, your stone will become stained from the juices and sauces in your pizzas. RESIST the urge to wash it with soap & water.

To clean your stone, uses a wire brush to scrub off any stuck on bits, and then bake your stone clean for up to 24 hours.

How to Cook a Pizza without a Pizza Stone

You can use:

Parchment paper

Cookie sheet

Specialty pizza pan

Directions:

Move oven rack to center position. Preheat oven to 450˚F.

Hand stretch or roll out pizza crust on lightly greased cookie sheet. If you're using a non-stick specialty pizza pan then you won't need any additional grease or cooking spray.

Bake pizza for 6-8 minutes, rotating the pizza 180˚ once, halfway through cooking. (The back of your oven is always hotter than the front, so rotate the pizza for even baking.

Broil if needed.

Slice & serve pizza.

One other important tip...

If you're using parchment paper, make sure that the paper doesn't touch the walls of your oven because it will cause excessive heat and your pizza will likely burn.

How to Grill a Pizza

Grilled pizzas are quickly becoming one of the fastest growing trends in the market, for best results all grilled pizzas should be thin crust and sparsely topped.

Preheat your BBQ to 400°F

Slap or roll out your small dough patty (8oz) to between 1/8" to ¼" thick

Poke with a fork several times

Gently lay crust onto grill, close lid & grill for 2 minutes

Flip crust, close lid & grill for 2 minutes

Remove crust from grill

Lightly top crust with cheese, grilled vegetables and meats

Lay pizza on grill, close lid and grill for 2-4 minutes or until cheese is melted.

Remove pizza from grill, slice & serve

A note about the dough recipes:

The specified weights are for what's considered a 'medium thickness of pizza crust'. If you prefer thin, use the smaller portioned dough balls for all your recipes. Conversely, if you prefer 'thick' style, simply divide the recipe into fewer balls. Your cook times and techniques will vary slightly; thinner crusts will cook quicker, thicker crusts may need an extra minute or two in the oven.

Moosehead™ Beer Dough Recipe

Approximate yield – 4 Medium (13 oz) dough patties or 2 Medium (13 oz) & 4 Small (8 oz)

- 1 ½ cup Moosehead™ Beer
- 1 cup water (lukewarm temperature 72°F)
- 2 tsp Celtic Sea Salt ® or Nature's Cargo Sea Salt ™
- 2 tsp sugar
- 16 g Yeast (which is 2 packages of Fleishman's' instant active dry yeast)
- 2 tbsp Extra Virgin Olive Oil
- 1000 g (6 cups) unbleached white flour (all purpose)

Dissolve sugar and salt in water/beer mixture (use Wisk). TIP: it helps if the water is warmed up. Temperature of the water should be between 95°F - 105°F. Add flour and mix on low speed for 3 minutes Stop mixer; add oil and yeast and mix on low speed for another 3 minutes. Stop mixer, mix on high speed for another 3 minutes. Total mixing time 9 minutes.

Weigh out dough in four - 13 oz or (370g) for medium dough patties (12" pizza). Roll into balls – but careful not to over work the dough (it'll make the pizza tough). Cover and put in your fridge for 24-36 hours to proof (rise).

Please note: I can't make a batch this small in my pizza dough mixer at the shop, so I use a heavy duty Kitchen aid Stand Mixer, or I mix it by hand. Pizza dough is very heavy compared to bread dough, and the beer in the recipe adds a little extra weight. If you don't have a heavy duty stand mixer, I'd recommend mixing by hand.

Make extra for next time...

Save yourself some time and double up your batch. Wrap the extra dough balls in Saran Wrap, then a freezer grade Ziploc bag and freeze immediately. Store your frozen dough in your freezer for up to 4 months. When you're ready to use your dough, either leave them on your counter for 3 hours to proof, or overnight in the fridge and they're ready to use for the next day. Use a patty for breadsticks with a pasta dish, or better yet, they're great with the lasagna stuffed red peppers on page 57.

Honey Wheat Moosehead™ Beer Dough

Approximate yield – 4 Medium (13 oz) dough patties or 2 Medium (13 oz) & 4 Small (8 oz)

- 400 g white flour
- 600 g whole wheat flour
- 2 cups Moosehead™ Lager Beer
- ½ cup water
- 2 tsp Nature's Cargo Sea Salt ™
- 4 tbsp Honey – John Russell Honey
- 2 tbsp Extra Virgin Olive Oil
- 16 g yeast (2 packages)

Dissolve sugar and salt in water/beer mixture (use Wisk). TIP: it helps if the water is warmed up. Temperature of the water should be between 95°F - 105°F. Add flour and mix on low speed for 3 minutes Stop mixer; add oil and yeast and mix on low speed for another 3 minutes Stop mixer; mix on high speed for another 3 minutes. Total mixing time 9 minutes.

Weigh out dough into 4 Medium (13 oz) or (370g) dough patties or 2 Medium (13 oz) & 4 Small (8 oz) or (225g). Roll into balls – but careful not to over work the dough or it will be tough. Cover and put in your fridge for 24-36 hours to proof (rise).

Please note: I use a heavy duty Kitchen aid Stand Mixer to make this batch size, or I mix it by hand. Pizza dough is very heavy compared to bread dough, and the beer in the recipe adds a little extra weight. If you don't have a heavy duty stand mixer, I'd recommend mixing by hand.

Whole Wheat Dough

Approximate yield – 4 Medium (13 oz) or (370g) dough patties or 2 Medium (13 oz) & 4 Small (8 oz) or (225g)

- 1000 g (6 cups) whole wheat flour (fine grind)
- 2 ½ cups water
- 2 tsp Sea Salt
- 2 tsp Sugar
- 2 tbsp Extra Virgin Olive Oil
- 16 g yeast (2 packages)

Dissolve salt and sugar in water (use Wisk). TIP: it helps if the water is warmed up. Temperature of the water should be between 95°F - 105°F. Add flour to water & mix on low speed for 2 minutes. Stop mixer, and let dough sit for ½ hour to allow the wheat to hydrate with the water. After ½ hour, add oil and yeast and mix on low speed for another 2 minutes. Stop mixer, mix on high speed for another 2 minutes. Total mixing time 6-7 minutes.

Weigh out dough into 4 Medium (13 oz) dough patties or 2 Medium (13 oz) & 4 Small (8 oz). Roll into balls – but careful not to over work the dough or it will be tough. Cover your dough and proof in fridge overnight. Note: if rapid proofing is needed, allow dough to rise (covered) at room temperature for 30 -60 minutes.

Marinara Sauce

- 1 (680ml/ 22 fl. oz) can Grade 'A' crushed tomatoes
- 1 ½ tsp Oregano
- 1 ½ tsp Basil
- ½ tbsp Fresh minced Garlic
- ½ tsp Nature's Cargo Sea Salt ™
- 1 ½ tsp Sugar
- ¾ tsp Pepper

Blend spices well into tomatoes, using a medium sauce pot. Cover & let simmer over low heat for 15 minutes OR blend spices well into tomatoes, cover & let marinate overnight in your refrigerator.

Olive Oil & Herb Sauce

- Extra Virgin Olive oil
- ½ tsp Oregano
- ½ tsp Basil
- ½ tsp Minced Garlic
- 1 tsp Nature's Cargo Sea Salt ™
- Pepper

Salsa

Use your favourite salsa instead of marinara for a whole different flavour. We use a Fire roasted Jalapeno pepper salsa from Sysco in 100 oz cans and drain about 1 &1/2 cups of liquid and it's amazing on pizza! If you don't drain the excess liquid, it will seep into your crust and give you a real soggy pizza, with what's known in the industry as an excessive gum line; the portion of the crust directly under the sauce will always be a little 'doughy', but if your sauce is too watery, the pizza won't bake up properly and will have more gum line than crust and likely make the pizza taste like raw dough.

Pesto

Use either homemade or store bought pesto for a dynamic flavour on your pizzas.

- 1 tsp sea salt
- 4 Cloves Garlic
- 2 cups (lightly packed) fresh Basil leaves
- 2 tbsp toasted pine nuts – delicately toasted in a hot preheated pan for 3-4 minutes (stirring constantly) or until lightly browned.
- ½ cup extra virgin Olive Oil
- ½ cup freshly grated parmesan cheese

In a food processor fitted with the metal blade, process the garlic & salt until minced. Next add the basil, olive oil & pine nuts and mix until smooth. Add the Parmesan and 'pulse' for 1-2 minutes. Use immediately or store in the refrigerator in a covered container for up to 2 weeks. You may store in the freezer for up to 3 months.

Honey Wheat Moosehead™ Beer Crust with Roasted Red Peppers, Seasoned Chicken Breast & Black Olives

- One Honey Wheat Moosehead Beer dough ball (already proofed)
- 1 tsp minced garlic
- 1 tsp oregano
- 1 tsp basil
- Dash of sea salt & pepper
- 2 Chicken breasts
- 6 oz Marinara
- 2 Red peppers
- ½ cup black olives, sliced & drained

Heat a 12" frying pan over medium heat then add 1 tbsp of olive oil. Heat oil for 2 minutes then add 2 chicken breasts (slice breast into ¼ inch strips, approximately ¾ inch long), minced garlic, oregano, basil & a sprinkle of pepper & sea salt. Cover & cook over low to medium heat until thoroughly cooked. Once finished, set aside for later use.

Core & slice red peppers into ¼ inch slices. Spray a 9"x 9" cake pan with non stick cooking spray. Sprinkle sea salt on red pepper slices and roast at 450°F for 12 minutes. Toss gently half way through cooking.

Hand slap (or use a rolling pin) the medium dough patty onto a 12" pizza screen. Spread 2-3oz of marinara sauce which was previously set aside. Add sliced seasoned chicken then smother with 6 oz mozzarella cheese. Top with roasted red peppers and sliced black olives – rule of thumb - a little in every bite. Bake in preheated oven at 450°F for 7-9 minutes or until golden brown. Slice & serve.

Chicken Parmigiana on a Moosehead™ Beer Crust

- 1 (13 oz) or (370g) Moosehead Beer dough patty (already proofed)
- 6 oz marinara sauce
- 6 oz 100% white breaded chicken cutlets, cut into bit size pieces and spread evenly throughout the pizza (chicken must be almost fully cooked before putting on the pizza)
  8 oz low fat part skim mozzarella, grated (cheese on top)
- pinch of oregano
- pinch of basil

Hand slap out (or use a rolling pin) dough patty on to 12" size pizza screen. Spread marinara sauce evenly on pizza, making sure you can't see any dough through the sauce. Spread out the breaded chicken cutlets which have been cut into bite size pieces. Smother with mozzarella cheese, then, sprinkle a pinch of oregano and basil on top. Bake in a conventional oven at 450° F for 7-9 minutes or until the crust and cheese are golden brown. See baking with or without a pizza stone.

Remove pizza from oven upon completion of cooking, slice into 8 pieces, serve immediately.

The Meatball Pie

Pepperoni, All Beef Meatballs on a Moosehead™ Beer Crust

- 1 (13 oz) or (370g) Moosehead dough patty (already proofed)
- 4 oz marinara sauce – see recipe below
- 2 oz dry cured pepperoni
- 8 - ½ oz 100% lean ground beef meatballs –spread evenly throughout the pizza (meatballs must be fully cooked then cut in half before putting on the pizza)
- 5 oz low fat part skim mozzarella, grated (cheese on top)
  3 oz medium sharp cheddar cheese, grated

Hand slap out dough patty on to 12" size pizza screen. Spread marinara sauce evenly on pizza. Sprinkle about 1 oz of cheese over the sauce. Place pepperoni in a circular pattern. Spread out the meatballs. Smother with mozzarella & cheddar cheeses. Bake in a conventional oven either using a pizza stone (see How to cook with a Pizza Stone) – OR preheat oven to 450˚ F and bake for 7-9 minutes or until the crust and cheese are golden brown.

Remove pizza from oven upon completion of cooking, slice into 8 pieces, serve immediately.

Pepperoni, Chicken Fingers and Jalapeno's on a Moosehead™ Beer Crust

A Trailer Park Boys™ inspired pizza

- 1 (13 oz) or (370g) Moosehead dough patty (already proofed)
- 4 oz marinara sauce
- 2 oz dry cured pepperoni
- 6 oz 100% white breaded chicken cutlets, cut into bit size pieces and spread evenly throughout the pizza (chicken must be fully cooked before putting on the pizza)
- 4-10 slices of Jalapeno peppers (depending on level of spice, for mild, break apart 3 Jalapenos and spread evenly on pizza – for really spicy, leave slices whole and place evenly on pizza)
- 5 oz low fat part skim mozzarella, grated (cheese on top) 3 oz medium sharp cheddar cheese, grated
- pinch of herbs (oregano & basil)

Hand slap out dough patty on to 12" size pizza screen. Spread marinara sauce evenly on pizza. Sprinkle about 1 oz of cheese over the sauce. Place pepperoni in a circular pattern. Spread out the breaded chicken cutlets which have been cut into bite size pieces. Top pizza with Jalapeno's according to your spicy preference. Smother with mozzarella & cheddar cheeses, then, sprinkle a pinch of oregano and basil on top. Bake in a conventional oven either using a pizza stone (see How to cook with a Pizza Stone) –OR preheat oven to 450∘ F and bake for 7-9 minutes or until the crust and cheese are golden brown. Broil if needed.

Remove pizza from oven upon completion of cooking, slice into 8 pieces, serve immediately.

Capicolla Ham, Broccoli with Mozzarella & Cheddar Cheeses

- 1 (13 oz) or (370g) dough patty (already proofed)
- Olive oil
- ½ tsp Oregano
- ½ tsp Basil
- ½ tsp Minced Garlic (dried- or 2 cloves fresh)
- 1 tsp Nature's Cargo Sea Salt ™
- Pepper
- 2 oz Capicolla ham sliced
- 1 cup of broccoli flowerets, washed & broken into bite size pieces
- 4 oz low fat mozzarella cheese, grated
- 2 oz medium sharp cheddar cheese, grated

Hand slap out dough patty on to 12" size pizza screen. Brush center of pizza (where you would normally spread red sauce) with olive oil. Sprinkle oregano, basil, minced garlic, sea salt and pepper on crust. Sprinkle about 1 oz of cheese over the sauce. Then using the rule of 'a little in every bite' top pizza with Capicolla ham & Broccoli. Smother with mozzarella & cheddar cheeses. Bake in a conventional oven either using a pizza stone (see How to cook with a Pizza Stone) –OR preheat oven to 450◦ F and bake for 7-9 minutes or until the crust and cheese are golden brown.

Remove pizza from oven upon completion of cooking, slice into 8 pieces, serve immediately.

Healthy Pizza

Lightly Seasoned Chicken Breast, Spinach, Red Peppers, Asparagus and Sundried Tomatoes with Mozzarella Cheese on a Whole Wheat Crust

- 1 medium (13oz) or (370g) whole wheat dough patty
- 4 oz marinara sauce –use a thick pasta sauce with low sodium
- 2 oz Chicken Breast – fully cooked, diced
- 1/8 package of frozen spinach – slightly thawed, drained
- 4 Asparagus spears – frozen also works well, cut into bite size pieces
- 1 red pepper, sliced ¼" rings
- ½ cup of sundried tomatoes, sliced julienne style – rinsed well under hot water to remove excess salt and drained. For best results, rinse for 5 minutes and let soak for 1 hour (or overnight) before using. This will remove a lot of the salt, allowing the natural sweetness of the tomatoes to come out and also will re-hydrate the sundried tomatoes just enough so they won't burn in the oven.
- pinch of herbs (oregano, basil, sea salt, pepper and minced garlic)
- splash of Extra virgin olive oil
- 5 oz low fat mozzarella cheese – look for 15-19% milk fat

Toss sliced chicken breast in a bowl with a splash of olive oil & a sprinkle of the herbs above. Using a cookie sheet, bake chicken breast in a preheated oven at 350'F for 20-25 minutes or until chicken is fully cooked – do not overcook. Set aside to cool before dicing into bite size pieces. Hand slap out dough patty on to 12" size pizza screen. Spread marinara sauce evenly on pizza. Smother with mozzarella cheese. Then using the rule of 'a little in every bite' top pizza with seasoned chicken, red peppers, spinach (squeeze out excess water before topping), asparagus and sundried tomatoes. Bake in a conventional oven either using a pizza stone (see How to cook with a Pizza Stone) –OR preheat oven to 450° F and bake for 7-9 minutes or until the crust and cheese are golden brown. Broil if needed.

Remove pizza from oven upon completion of cooking, slice into 8 pieces. Serve immediately.

This is a very popular pizza on our menu, one of my favourites, lots of veggies and a little salty from the feta cheese

Greek Pizza

Italian Sausage, Green Peppers, Red Onions, Black Olives, Roma Tomatoes with Feta and Mozzarella Cheeses

- 1 (13 oz) dough patty (already proofed)
- 5 oz Marinara
- 3 oz Italian Sausage – fully cooked, diced
- ½ green pepper, sliced
- ½ red onion, sliced
- 2 Roma tomato, sliced
- ¼ cup slice black olives
- 5 oz low fat mozzarella cheese, grated
- 3 oz crumbled feta cheese

Hand slap out dough patty on to 12" size pizza screen. Spread Marinara sauce evenly on pizza. Smother with mozzarella. Then using the rule of 'a little in every bite' top pizza with sliced tomatoes, sliced green peppers, black olives and the sliced red onions. Spread Italian sausage evenly on pizza. Bake in a conventional oven either using a pizza stone (see How to cook with a Pizza Stone) –OR preheat oven to 450° F and bake for 7-9 minutes or until the crust and cheese are golden brown.

Remove pizza from oven upon completion of cooking, slice into 8 pieces, serve immediately.

Healthy Pizza

Greek Pizza

This pizza was awarded "Canada's Pizza of the year 2006" by Canadian Pizza magazine

Big D's Bodacious BLT on a Moosehead™ Beer Crust

- 1 (8 oz) Moosehead dough patty (already proofed)
- 5 oz low fat mozzarella cheese, grated
- 3 oz Medium sharp Cheddar cheese, grated
- 3 oz Canadian Back Bacon
- 2.5 oz Canadian Side Bacon (crumbled)
- Celtic Sea Salt ® or Nature's Cargo Sea Salt ™ and pepper to taste
- 3 Roma tomatoes, diced
- 1 head romaine lettuce, washed and diced/shredded (prep like you would for tacos or wraps)
- Sunspun™ Ranch Dressing

Hand slap out dough patty on to 12" size pizza screen. This is a NO SAUCE pizza. Top with mozzarella & cheddar cheese, then using the rule of 'a little in every bite' top Back Bacon, & crumbled Bacon. Bake in a conventional oven either using a pizza stone (see How to cook with a Pizza Stone) –OR preheat oven to 450° F and bake for 7-9 minutes or until the crust and cheese are golden brown.

Remove pizza from oven upon completion of cooking, slice into 8 pieces, then top with diced Roma tomatoes, sea salt & pepper, drizzle with ranch dressing, top with shredded romaine lettuce and finally sprinkle a little more sea salt, pepper and another drizzle of ranch dressing. Serve immediately.

Matt's Mix

Spicy Chipotle Pesto, Capicolla Ham, Cajun Chicken, Mushrooms, Red Peppers and Mozzarella & Monterey Jack Cheeses

- 1 (13 oz) dough patty (already proofed)
- 5 oz Spicy Chipotle Pesto Sauce
- 2 oz 100% white chicken breast – fully cooked, diced
- 2 oz Capicolla ham sliced
- 1 red pepper, sliced
- sliced fresh mushrooms
- 3 oz low fat mozzarella cheese, grated
- 2.5 oz Monterey jack cheese, grated

Hand slap out dough patty on to 12" size pizza screen. Spread chipotle sauce evenly on pizza. Smother with mozzarella, cheddar & Monterey jack cheeses. Then using the rule of 'a little in every bite' top pizza with strip bacon, diced tomatoes, diced red & green peppers and the diced onions. In a separate bowl, toss diced chicken with Frank's Hot Sauce. Spread chicken evenly on pizza. Bake in a conventional oven either using a pizza stone (see How to cook with a Pizza Stone) –OR preheat oven to 450° F and bake for 7-9 minutes or until the crust and cheese are golden brown.

Remove pizza from oven upon completion of cooking, slice into 8 pieces, serve immediately.

Big D's Bodacious BLT on a Beer Crust

South West Chipotle Combo

This is one of my favourite pizzas, lots of veggies, a little bit of meat, a little spicy and loads of flavour.

South West Chipotle Combo

Spicy Chipotle Pesto, Cajun Chicken, Strip Bacon, Red & Green Peppers, Red Onions and Roma Tomatoes with Cheddar, Mozzarella & Monterey Jack Cheeses

- 1 (13 oz) dough patty (already proofed)
- 5 oz Spicy Chipotle Pesto Sauce
- 2 oz 100% white chicken breast – fully cooked, diced
- 2 oz strip bacon – fully cooked, diced
- 1 tblsp Frank's Hot Sauce
- 1 green pepper, diced
- 1 red pepper, diced
- ½ red onion, diced
- 2 Roma tomato, sliced
- 3 oz low fat mozzarella cheese, grated
- 2.5 oz medium sharp cheddar cheese, grated
- 2.5 oz Monterey jack cheese, grated

Hand slap out dough patty on to 12" size pizza screen. Spread chipotle sauce evenly on pizza. Smother with mozzarella, cheddar & Monterey jack cheeses. Then using the rule of 'a little in every bite' top pizza with strip bacon, sliced tomatoes, diced red & green peppers and the diced onions. In a separate bowl, toss diced chicken with Frank's Hot Sauce. Spread chicken evenly on pizza. Bake in a conventional oven either using a pizza stone (see How to cook with a Pizza Stone) –OR preheat oven to 450° F and bake for 7-9 minutes or until the crust and cheese are golden brown.

Remove pizza from oven upon completion of cooking, slice into 8 pieces, serve immediately.

This is another one of my favourite pizzas, it's a little sloppy, but just one bite and you'll be willing to put up with the mess.

Spicy Taco Pizza

- 1 (13 oz) or (370g) dough patty (already proofed)
- 5 oz Fire Roasted Jalapeno and Red Pepper Salsa (you will need to drain most of the liquid off)
- 3 oz cooked lean ground beef, seasoned with taco mix
- ¼ cup black olives
- 2 Roma tomato, sliced
- 4-10 slices of Jalapeno peppers (depending on level of spice, for mild, break apart 3 Jalapenos and spread evenly on pizza – for really spicy, leave slices whole and place evenly on pizza)
- Sunspun™ Ranch Dressing
- 1 tbsp Frank's Hot Sauce
- 3 oz low fat mozzarella cheese, grated
- 2.5 oz medium sharp cheddar cheese, grated
- 2.5 oz Monterey jack cheese, grated
- 1 cup Taco chips, crushed
- 3 cups Romaine lettuce, shredded

Hand slap out dough patty on to 12" size pizza screen. Spread salsa sauce evenly on pizza. Then using the rule of 'a little in every bite' top pizza with black olives, sliced tomatoes and the jalapenos. In a separate bowl, toss beef with Frank's Hot Sauce. Spread taco beef evenly on pizza. Drizzle ranch dressing over all the toppings. Smother with mozzarella, cheddar & Monterey jack cheeses. Bake in a conventional oven either using a pizza stone (see How to cook with a Pizza Stone) – OR preheat oven to 450° F and bake for 7-9 minutes or until the crust and cheese are golden brown.

Remove pizza from oven upon completion of cooking, slice into 8 pieces, top with crushed taco chips and fresh lettuce. Serve immediately.

Taco Pizza

- 1 (13 oz) dough patty (already proofed)
- 5 oz Fire Roasted Jalapeno and Red Pepper Salsa (you will need to drain most of the liquid off)
- 3 oz cooked lean ground beef, seasoned with taco mix
- ¼ cup black olives
- 2 Roma tomato, sliced
- Sunspun™ Ranch Dressing
- 3 oz low fat mozzarella cheese, grated
- 2.5 oz medium sharp cheddar cheese, grated
- 2.5 oz Monterey jack cheese, grated
- 1 cup Taco chips, crushed
- 3 cups Romaine lettuce, shredded

Hand slap out dough patty on to 12" size pizza screen. Spread salsa sauce evenly on pizza. Then using the rule of 'a little in every bite' top pizza with black olives and sliced tomatoes. In a separate bowl, toss beef with Frank's Hot Sauce. Spread taco beef evenly on pizza. Drizzle ranch dressing over all the toppings. Smother with mozzarella, cheddar & Monterey jack cheeses. Bake in a conventional oven either using a pizza stone (see How to cook with a Pizza Stone) –OR preheat oven to 450° F and bake for 7-9 minutes or until the crust and cheese are golden brown.

Remove pizza from oven upon completion of cooking, slice into 8 pieces, top with crushed taco chips and fresh lettuce. Serve immediately.

Telly's Special

Teriyaki Chicken Breast, Roasted Red Peppers and Pineapple with Mozzarella Cheese

- 1 (13 oz) dough patty (already proofed)
- 4 oz marinara
- 2 oz 100% white chicken breast – fully cooked, diced
- 3 oz pineapple (canned tidbits, or fresh sliced into bite size pieces)
- 2 red peppers, sliced ¼"
- 5 oz low fat mozzarella cheese

Preheat oven to 450° F. Drizzle red pepper slices with olive oil & herbs. Spread out on cookie sheet & bake for 15-20 minutes or until edges are blackened.

Hand slap out dough patty on to 12" size pizza screen. Spread marinara sauce evenly on pizza. Smother with mozzarella cheese. Then using the rule of 'a little in every bite' top pizza with roasted red peppers and pineapple. In a separate bowl, toss diced chicken with Teriyaki Sauce. Spread chicken evenly on pizza. Bake in a conventional oven either using a pizza stone (see How to cook with a Pizza Stone) – OR preheat oven to 450° F and bake for 7-9 minutes or until the crust and cheese are golden brown.

Remove pizza from oven upon completion of cooking, slice into 8 pieces, serve immediately.

This pizza was entered in the 'Pizza Classica' competition in Italy by my friends Dale & Fran from the Irish Pizza Team. It was awarded 'Best Pizza in Ireland 2006' by the judges. The fellow who created this pizza is named Michael, and a member of the Irish Pizza Team, but he was too shy to enter the competition himself. I got to taste a sliver and it was fabulous! Of course I shared my award winning Moosehead Beer dough recipe with them so they could make it with Guinness then top it with this specialty pie.

The Michelangelo Pizza

- 1 (13 oz) dough patty (already proofed)
- 5 oz Marinara
- 5 oz mozzarella, grated
- 3 oz Pepperoni
- ½ red onion, sliced (caramelized)
- 4 oz goat cheese, sliced in small centimeter cubes
- 2 oz pesto sauce

Hand slap out dough patty on to 12" size pizza screen. In a frying pan, cook onions over low heat with a little olive oil until they darken and soften. Spread Marinara sauce evenly on pizza. Smother with mozzarella. Then using the rule of 'a little in every bite' top pizza with pepperoni and sliced caramelized onions. Add a few dollops of pesto sauce on top. Place goat cheese cubes opposite dollops of pesto. Bake in a conventional oven either using a pizza stone (see How to cook with a Pizza Stone) –OR preheat oven to 450° F and bake for 7-9 minutes or until the crust and cheese are golden brown.

Remove pizza from oven upon completion of cooking, slice into 8 pieces, serve immediately.

Light & tasty, this pizza is best served on a thin crust. One tip when using sun-dried tomatoes on a pizza is that you need to rinse them in hot water and soak them, preferably overnight. Otherwise they'll burn quickly and ruin a great pizza.

The Californian

Olive Oil & Herb Sauce, Lightly Seasoned Chicken Breast, Sun-dried Tomatoes, Diced Roma Tomatoes & Red Onions.

- 1 (13 oz) dough patty (already proofed)
- Olive oil
- ½ tsp Oregano
- ½ tsp Basil
- ½ tsp Minced Garlic (dried- or 2 cloves fresh)
- 1 tsp Nature's Cargo Sea Salt ™
- Pepper
- ½ red onion, sliced
- 2 Roma tomato, diced
- 1/3 cup sun-dried tomatoes, sliced, rinsed & soaked
- 2 oz 100% white chicken breast – fully cooked, diced
- 5 oz low fat mozzarella cheese, grated

Hand slap out dough patty on to 12" size pizza screen. Combine dried herbs in a shaker for easy application. Brush center of pizza (where you would normally spread red sauce) with olive oil. Sprinkle oregano, basil, minced garlic, sea salt and pepper on crust. Combine red onions, diced chicken, sun-dried and diced Roma tomatoes in a bowl and marinate with 2 tsp of olive oil & a good sprinkle of the herbs. Mix well. Spread out topping mixture on pizza. Smother with mozzarella cheese. Bake in a conventional oven either using a pizza stone (see How to cook with a Pizza Stone) –OR preheat oven to 450° F and bake for 7-9 minutes or until the crust and cheese are golden brown.

Remove pizza from oven upon completion of cooking, and then slice into 8 pieces. Serve immediately.

This is a great pizza, light and has a nice slight spice to it, and with so many veggies, you shouldn't feel the least bit guilty! One tip for using spinach on pizzas, buy frozen spinach and allow it to thaw. Then make sure to squeeze any excess water from it before putting it on the pizza.

D's Delight

Olive Oil & Herb Sauce, Cajun Chicken, Red Peppers, Spinach, Roma Tomatoes with Mozzarella Cheese

- 1 (13 oz) dough patty (already proofed)
- Olive oil
- ½ tsp Oregano
- ½ tsp Basil
- ½ tsp Minced Garlic
- 1 tsp Nature's Cargo Sea Salt ™
- Pepper
- 2 oz 100% white chicken breast – fully cooked, diced
- 1tblsp Frank's Hot Sauce
- 1 red pepper, sliced ¼" rings
- 2 Roma tomato, sliced
- ¼ package of frozen spinach, thawed
- 5 oz low fat mozzarella cheese

In a separate bowl, toss diced chicken with Frank's Hot Sauce. Hand slap out dough patty on to 12" size pizza screen. Brush center of pizza (where you would normally spread red sauce) with olive oil. Sprinkle oregano, basil, minced garlic, sea salt and pepper on crust. Smother with mozzarella cheese. Then using the rule of 'a little in every bite' top pizza with Cajun chicken, red peppers and Roma tomatoes. Squeeze out excess water from spinach before you place it on the pizza. Bake in a conventional oven either using a pizza stone (see How to cook with a Pizza Stone) –OR preheat oven to 450° F and bake for 7-9 minutes or until the crust and cheese are golden brown.

Remove pizza from oven upon completion of cooking, slice into 8 pieces. Serve immediately.

The Couch Potato

Olive Oil & Herb Sauce, Seasoned Wedge Fries, Teriyaki Fried Onions, Strip Bacon, Seasoned Beef with a Havarti Garlic Chive Cheese Blend

- 1 (13 oz) dough patty (already proofed)
- Olive oil
- ½ tsp Oregano
- ½ tsp Basil
- ½ tsp Minced Garlic
- 1 tsp Nature's Cargo Sea Salt ™
- Pepper
- ¼ lb Seasoned Wedge Fries – fully cooked, cut into bite size pieces
- 3 oz strip bacon – fully cooked, diced
- 2 oz cooked lean ground beef, seasoned with taco mix
- ½ red onion, sliced
- 2 tbsp Teriyaki Sauce
- Sunspun™ Ranch Dressing
- 3 oz low fat mozzarella cheese, grated
- 2 oz Havarti Garlic Chive cheese, grated

In a small frying pan, cook onions over low heat with the Teriyaki sauce. Hand slap out dough patty on to 12" size pizza screen. Brush center of pizza (where you would normally spread red sauce) with olive oil. Sprinkle oregano, basil, minced garlic, sea salt and pepper on crust. Then using the rule of 'a little in every bite' top pizza with wedge fries, strip bacon, teriyaki fried onions and the seasoned beef. Smother with mozzarella & havarti cheeses. Bake in a conventional oven either using a pizza stone (see How to cook with a Pizza Stone) –OR preheat oven to 450◦ F and bake for 7-9 minutes or until the crust and cheese are golden brown.

Remove pizza from oven upon completion of cooking, drizzle ranch dressing over entire pizza, then slice into 8 pieces. Serve immediately.

BBQ Chicken Pizza

BBQ Sauce, BBQ Chicken breast, Strip Bacon, Red Onions with Mozzarella & Cheddar Cheeses

- 1 (13 oz) dough patty (already proofed)
- 4 oz BBQ Sauce (I like Diana Brand name sauce, Honey-Garlic BBQ)
- 4 oz 100% white chicken breast – fully cooked, diced
- 2 oz strip bacon – fully cooked, diced
- ¼ red onion, sliced
- 3 oz low fat mozzarella cheese, grated
- 2.5 oz medium sharp cheddar cheese, grated

Hand slap out dough patty on to 12" size pizza screen. Spread BBQ sauce evenly on pizza. Smother with mozzarella and cheddar cheeses. Then using the rule of 'a little in every bite' top pizza with strip bacon and red onion. In a separate bowl, toss chicken with Diana BBQ Sauce. Spread chicken evenly on pizza. Bake in a conventional oven either using a pizza stone (see How to cook with a Pizza Stone) –OR preheat oven to 450° F and bake for 7-9 minutes or until the crust and cheese are golden brown.

Remove pizza from oven upon completion of cooking, slice into 8 pieces. Serve immediately.

This is a very popular pizza, using one of my favourite meat toppings, Capicolla ham. Capicolla ham is a ham infused with a red pepper sauce and you'll find mildly spiced to crazy 'monkey butt' hot types. The mushrooms will dampen the spice a bit, but they also add their own element of flavour to this pie.

Italian Pizza

Capicolla Ham, Green Peppers, Fresh Mushrooms, Black Olives with Oregano & Basil

- 1 (13 oz) dough patty (already proofed)
- 5 oz Marinara
- 5 oz Capicolla Ham – (your preference mildly spiced or fired up), sliced
- ½ green pepper, sliced
- ¼ cup sliced black olives
- 5 oz fresh mushrooms, sliced
- 5 oz low fat mozzarella cheese, grated
- Oregano
- Basil

Hand slap out dough patty on to 12" size pizza screen. Spread Marinara sauce evenly on pizza. Smother with mozzarella. Then using the rule of 'a little in every bite' top pizza with sliced Capicolla Ham, sliced green peppers, mushrooms and the black olives. Sprinkle (lightly) oregano and basil evenly on pizza. Bake in a conventional oven either using a pizza stone (see How to cook with a Pizza Stone) –OR preheat oven to 450 °F and bake for 7-9 minutes or until the crust and cheese are golden brown.

Remove pizza from oven upon completion of cooking, slice into 8 pieces, serve immediately.

The Californian

BBQ Chicken Pizza

The Breakfast Pizza

Salsa, Capicolla Ham, Sliced Hard Boiled Egg with Mozzarella, Monterey & Cheddar Cheeses

- 1 (13 oz) dough patty (already proofed)
- 5 oz Fire Roasted Jalapeno and Red Pepper Salsa (you will need to drain most of the liquid off)
- 2 oz Capicolla ham sliced
- 2 hard boiled eggs, sliced
- 4 oz low fat part skim mozzarella, grated (cheese on top)
  3 oz medium sharp cheddar cheese, grated
- 2 oz Monterey jack cheese, grated

Hand slap out dough patty on to 12" size pizza screen. Spread salsa sauce evenly on pizza. Sprinkle about 3 oz of cheese over the sauce. Place the Capicolla ham in a circular pattern. Spread out sliced hard boiled eggs. Smother with remaining mozzarella & cheddar cheeses. Bake in a conventional oven either using a pizza stone (see How to cook with a Pizza Stone) –OR preheat oven to 450 ∘F and bake for 7-9 minutes or until the crust and cheese are golden brown.

Remove pizza from oven upon completion of cooking, slice into 8 pieces, serve immediately.

Chicken Fiesta Pizza on a Moosehead™ Beer Crust

- 1 (13 oz) Moosehead™ dough patty (already proofed)
- 5 oz Casa Solana™ Fire Roasted Jalapeno Salsa (Sysco brand)
- 2 oz 100% white chicken breast – fully cooked, diced
- 1 can of corn kernels, rinsed (only need approximately 2 tbsp)
- 1 can of black beans, rinsed (only need approximately 2 tbsp)
- 1 green pepper, diced
- 1 Roma tomato, diced
- 3 oz black olives, sliced
- 6 Jalapeno pepper rings (pizza style), diced
- Extra Virgin Olive Oil (splash)
- pinch of oregano
- pinch of basil
- Celtic Sea Salt ® or Nature's Cargo Sea Salt ™ and pepper to taste
- 3 oz low fat mozzarella cheese, grated
- 2.5 oz medium sharp cheddar cheese, grated
- 2.5 oz Monterey jack cheese, grated

Hand slap out dough patty on to 12" size pizza screen. Spread salsa evenly on pizza. Smother with mozzarella, cheddar & Monterey jack cheeses. Then using the rule of 'a little in every bite' top with corn, black beans, diced tomatoes, diced Jalapeno & green peppers, black olives. In a separate bowl, toss diced chicken with a splash of olive oil and a sprinkle of oregano, basil, sea salt and pepper. Evenly top the chicken on the pizza. Bake in a conventional oven either using a pizza stone (see How to cook with a Pizza Stone) –OR preheat oven to 450° F and bake for 7-9 minutes or until the crust and cheese are golden brown.

Remove pizza from oven upon completion of cooking, slice into 8 pieces, serve immediately.

When the moon hits your eye like a big pizza pie, that's amore. I came up with this pizza after reading an article in Canadian Pizza Magazine. Historically, many favourite pizza toppings are known to contain sexual stimulant properties and researchers have found that the smell, taste & even appearance of foods not only get you in the mood, but also make you a better lover. A note of caution, sharing this pizza with the wrong individual may produce undesired results. I assume no responsibility for re-kindled unwanted romances, blame it on the pie!

Lip-Smackin' Libido Luster Buster

Oysters, Onions, Green & Black Olives, Artichoke Hearts & Garlic with Mozzarella Cheese

- 1 (13 oz) dough patty (already proofed)
- 5 oz Marinara
- 2 cloves of garlic, minced
- 1 tin oysters, broken up and spread out on pizza
- ¼ cup sliced black olives
- ¼ cup sliced green olives
- ½ red onion, sliced
- 1 jar of marinated artichoke hearts
- 5 oz low fat mozzarella cheese, grated

Hand slap out dough patty on to 12" size pizza screen. Spread Marinara sauce evenly on pizza. Smother with mozzarella. Then using the rule of 'a little in every bite' top pizza with oysters, black & green olives, sliced onions, and artichoke hearts. Sprinkle minced garlic evenly on pizza. Bake in a conventional oven either using a pizza stone (see How to cook with a Pizza Stone) –OR preheat oven to 450˚ F and bake for 7-9 minutes or until the crust and cheese are golden brown.

Remove pizza from oven upon completion of cooking, slice into 8 pieces, serve immediately.

Award winning entrée recipe Italian Chef Wars 2006, Las Vegas NV. This recipe was part of a 3 course competition that I had 90 minutes to make in front of a live audience. I paired this with 'Big D's Bodacious BLT' and the Caramelized Cinnamon Honey Apples on a Honey Wheat Beer Crust Topped with Cinnamon & Honey Whipped Cream, both of which can also be found in this volume.

Lasagna Stuffed Red Peppers with Asparagus

- 4-8 Red Peppers (depending on size)
- 1 lbs asparagus
- 1 lbs. Lean Ground Beef
- 2 cups Marinara (see recipe)
- 2 cloves garlic, minced
- 1 cup shredded Romaine Lettuce
- 4 pieces lasagna noodles, broken into small bite-size pieces
- ½ lbs Mozzarella Cheese
- ½ lbs Havarti Garlic & Chive Cheese
- Parmesan Cheese
- Nature's Cargo Sea Salt ™
- Pepper
- Oregano
- Basil

Brown the beef over medium heat in a frying pan, making sure to break up ground beef in small pieces. Drain fat. Add minced garlic, a ½ tsp of dried oregano, ½ tsp of dried basil and a sprinkle of pepper & sea salt. Add shredded Romaine lettuce, mix in well. Add Marinara sauce & cook over low heat for 5 minutes.

Bring the water to boil in large pasta pot. Core red peppers, remove seeds and then cut peppers in half. Trim asparagus and cut tips 3"- 4" size pieces. Place red peppers (insides facing down) on a wire grate and place on top of pot (over boiling water) to steam for 10 minutes. Also, at this time, cook broken lasagna pieces (in same pot) according to directions.

Once the red peppers have steamed for 10 minutes, remove and allow to drip dry on a towel. Lightly sprinkle sea salt on inside of red peppers. Steam asparagus on wire grate on top of boiling water in same fashion as red peppers for 7-10 minutes. Drain pasta pieces & set aside.

Place red peppers halves (insides facing up) on a cookie sheet with a wire grate. Mix pasta pieces with meat sauce, then spoon a little in each red pepper half.

Add a layer of mozzarella & Havarti Garlic & Chive cheese, then spoon another layer of meat & pasta sauce in each half. If red peppers are large enough, repeat the layers. Top with layer of mozzarella & Havarti Garlic & Chive cheese and sprinkle oregano, basil, sea salt & parmesan cheese. Finally, place 3 asparagus tips on top of each stuffed pepper. Cover lightly with tin foil and bake in an oven at 400 ∘F for 30 minutes.

Dessert Pizzas

Caramelized Cinnamon Honey Apples on a Honey Wheat Beer Crust Topped with Cinnamon & Honey Whipped Cream

- 4-6 Granny Smith Apples
- 1/3 cup & 2 tbsp John Russell Honey
- 2 cups Heavy Whipping Cream
- 2 tbsp Cinnamon
- 2 tbsp butter
- ½ cup sugar
- 2 Small (8oz) Honey Wheat Moosehead Beer patties

Peel, core and slice apples into approximately ¼ inch wedges. Heat a medium frying pan to medium heat and add 1 tbsp of butter. Allow to melt, and then add sliced apples. Cook apples until a little soft (2-4 minutes), then add 2 tbsp of John Russell Honey, 1/3 cup of sugar & 1 tbsp cinnamon. Cook over low heat for 10-15 minutes or until apples are soft & caramelized. Remove from heat & set aside.

In a heavy duty stand mixer, whip 2 cups heavy whipping cream with 1/3 cup John Russell Honey & 1 tsp cinnamon until light & fluffy. Mix ¼ cup of sugar with 2 tsp of cinnamon & put in dredger for later use.

Slap or roll out small patties to 9" pizza screen. Pierce crust several times with a fork to eliminate bubbles while cooking. Brush crusts with 1 tbsp of melted butter, and then sprinkle with cinnamon sugar. Cook at 450°F for 10 minutes or until golden brown. Remove from oven, spoon warm cinnamon honey apples into center of crust. Top with fresh whipped cream & sprinkle with cinnamon sugar. Slice & serve warm.

Strawberry 'n Cream Cheese Sweet Roll with Chocolate Drizzle

- 1 pint strawberries, washed & sliced into 1/8" slices
- 1 package cream cheese, softened
- 1 tsp sugar
- 1 tsp cinnamon
- ½ package of Baker's chocolate
- 1 (13 oz) dough patty (already proofed)
- 1 tsp Nature's Cargo Sea Salt ™ -
- 2 tsp sugar
- 1 tbsp heavy cream
- 2 tbsp Extra Virgin Olive Oil
- 8 g yeast (1 package)

Hand Stretch (or use a rolling pin) the medium dough patty to a 12" x 12" square. Spread a thin layer of cream cheese on dough, leaving ½" around edges. Lay strawberries slices on top of cream cheese. Sprinkle sugar & cinnamon on top. Beginning at one side, roll edge tightly until completely rolled into log. Wet finger and seal edge of dough. Place on a cookie sheet with sealed edge down.

Bake in an oven at 450 °F for 15-20 minutes or until golden brown. When the sweet roll is almost finished baking, pour hot water from a kettle (or simply microwave water to heat up) in a small bowl. Place cubes of chocolate in Ziploc bag then in the hot water to allow chocolate to melt. Once the roll is baked to a golden brown, slice into 2" slices, garnish with whipped cream and slice of strawberry. Snip one corner of the Ziploc bag open with scissors, drizzle strawberry sweet roll slice with chocolate then serve.

Apple Pie Sundae Boat Topped with Whipped or Vanilla Ice Cream

- 1 cup Cinnamon Apple Pie Filling
- 2 tbsp Cinnamon
- 3 tbsp butter (melted)
- ¼ cup white sugar
- ¼ cup brown sugar
- 1 Small (8oz) dough patty

Combine cinnamon with both sugars & put in a dredger for easy application.

Hand stretch a small dough patty to 9" rectangle. Place on baking disk. Gently twist each end like a candy wrapper to create a 'boat' shape. Pierce crust several times with a fork to eliminate bubbles while cooking. Brush crust with 1 tbsp of melted butter, and then sprinkle with (a little) cinnamon sugar. Spoon cinnamon apple pie filling into center of crust, then sprinkle more cinnamon sugar on top.

Bake in an oven for 6-7 minutes or until golden brown. Top with fresh whipped cream (or ice cream). Slice & serve warm.

Recommended Reading

"The 5 Factor Diet" by Harley Pasternak
"You on a Diet" & "You: The Owner's Manual" by Dr's Michael Roizen & Mehmet Oz as seen on Oprah.
"Your Bodies Many Cries for Water" by F. Batmanghelidj M.D.

Musings – Observations about Life

I love to people watch. I find many funnies dealing with the public.

There's a regular who comes in to pick up his pizza and then tucks it sideways under his arm to carry it home. All the staff cringe at the sight of their hard work now unrecognizable and smashed against one side, but he & his wife must like it that way 'cuz he comes in every week.

Years ago we used to stay open until the wee hours of the morning. One very late night we had a girl who was ordering a pizza and kept saying "I have a coupon & I'd like to use it." Trying to clarify "which coupon?" repeatedly proved fruitless when she responded 'the one in my hand'. So my husband Pierre asked her to hold it up to the phone so he could read it. This was followed by several minutes of silence, although without a videophone we can't say for certain that she indeed held it up to the phone for him to read.

'Winnipeg's Dumbest Would Be Robber' - The would be robber who came in on the tail end of a Friday night supper shift with a 9" knife only to realize that he was outnumbered and we had more knives. Displaying two 15" knives, Crocodile Dundee style show-me-yours-I'll-show-you-mine 'That ain't a knife, THIS is a knife'. He ran away as 7 of our 'boys' chased him down the lane, cheered on by regulars across the street on their balcony yelling 'what happened' then 'kick his ass!' Apparently, the would-be robber could run faster scared than our boys could mad. He dove into a getaway car in a parking garage and it sped off. We like to think that although he didn't get the payload he expected, he did have a load in his pants by the time he got in the car. He hasn't been back.

Favourite dumb questions:
How much is free delivery?
What comes on your cheese pizza?

Does a large taste different than a medium?
Can I have green beef & peppers on that?
Can I get a vegetarian pizza with no pepperoni?
I want double strip bacon and triple pepperoni, but can you make sure it's not greasy?

More Observations...

You can tell a lot about the mentality of the place that you're in by the toilet paper in the washrooms. It's true, big businesses, small businesses, hotels, restaurants, even your best friend's place. You can totally size up a place by the quality of the toilet paper.

I've found 5 types, and it's not always the places that you'd expect so big tip here for the ladies is to always have tissues in your purse. Gentlemen, nature gave you an advantage when it comes to number 1, but for number 2, you're pretty much S.O.L. My only advice is to find a lady who's smart enough to carry tissues in her purse.

Sandpaper; self explanatory. But much preferred over...

Handpaper: also self explanatory. Both of these establishments are so tight on their nickels that they've hired an equally tight ass to squeeze every last penny out of the bottom line. Care level for employees and guests is -5. My sympathies if this happens to be your best friend.

1 ply. The tight ass couldn't order the above choice so he had to go with the next cheapest thing. Care level for employees and guests is 0

2ply. Someone with a brain uses the facilities. Care level for employees and guests is 5.

3ply. RARE. Someone made a mistake. Or someone has a sensitive hei-nie. Or someone really cares about the guests' experience, from beginning to end. Care level for employees and guests is 10. Bonus if this is your best friend.

Diana's Awards & Recognitions

"Canada's Best Non-Traditional Pizza 2009"
2009 International Pizza Challenge, Las Vegas, NV
Judge for 2009 World Pizza Championship Games – Salsomaggiore, Italy
Judge for 2009 "Coupe de France" (2009 French Pizza Competition)
Membre Honneur de la Fédération des Pizzaïolos de France
"Canada's Best Pizza Chef 2008"
2008 World Pizza Championship Games - Salsomaggiore, Italy
Ranked 20th in the World – 2008 World Pizza Cup Games, Naples Italy
Canada's 2008 Largest Stretch Champion - 2008 World Pizza Cup
Games, Naples Italy
"Canada's Best Pizza Chef 2007"
2007 World Pizza Olympic Games - Salsomaggiore, Italy
First Canadian Finalist for "Gourmet Pizza of the Year 2007"
Pizza Festiva Las Vegas, NV March 2007
"Canada's Pizza Chef of the Year 2005 & 2006"
Canadian Pizza Magazine
Canadian Finalist for "Italian Chef Wars 2005 & 2006"
Las Vegas, NV March 2005 & 2006
"World's 4th Best Pizza"
2005 America's Plate Culinary Competition, New York, NY
Coach of the Canadian Pizza Champions Team™
Featured columnist Canadian Pizza magazine
Honourary member of the World Pizza Champions Team™
Honourary member of the Australian Pizza Team™
Honourary member of the "Fédération des Pizzaïolos de France™"
Graduate of the official "Scuola Italiana Pizzaioli" June 2008
Guest Expert Speaker at the American Institute of Baking's "Pizza
Production Technology Course" 2007, 2008 & 2009
Featured columnist for Canadian Pizza Magazine
As seen on Glutton for Punishment on Canada's Food Network

In addition to creating award-winning recipes, Diana is also a consultant to other independent pizzeria owner/operators in menu development, creating systems to run a pizzeria on autopilot, along with marketing and positioning to help operators grow their business effectively and strategically. She is available for consulting on a limited basis, for more information contact her at Diana@dianasgourmetpizzeria.ca.

www.onegreatpizza.ca
Other websites of interest:
www.passionateaboutpizza.com
www.gourmetpizzeriasecrets.com